Before You Were Here, Mi Amor

by Samantha R. Vamos

illustrated by Santiago Cohen

VIKING

VIKING

Published by Penguin Group

Penguin Young Readers Group, 345 Hudson Street, New York, New York 10014, U.S.A.

Penguin Group (Canada), 90 Eglinton Avenue East, Suite 700, Toronto, Ontario, Canada M4P 2Y3

(a division of Pearson Penguin Canada Inc.)

Penguin Books Ltd, 80 Strand, London WC2R 0RL, England

Penguin Ireland, 25 St Stephen's Green, Dublin 2, Ireland (a division of Penguin Books Ltd)

Penguin Group (Australia), 250 Camberwell Road, Camberwell, Victoria 3124, Australia

(a division of Pearson Australia Group Pty Ltd)

Penguin Books India Pvt Ltd, 11 Community Centre, Panchsheel Park, New Delhi - 110 017, India

Penguin Group (NZ), 67 Apollo Drive, Rosedale, North Shore 0632, New Zealand

(a division of Pearson New Zealand Ltd)

Penguin Books (South Africa) (Pty) Ltd, 24 Sturdee Avenue, Rosebank, Johannesburg 2196, South Africa

Penguin Books Ltd, Registered Offices: 80 Strand, London WC2R 0RL, England

First published in 2009 by Viking, a division of Penguin Young Readers Group

10 9 8 7 6 5 4 3 2 1

Text copyright © Samantha R. Vamos, 2009
Illustrations copyright © Santiago Cohen, 2009

LIBRARY OF CONGRESS CATALOGING-IN-PUBLICATION DATA
Vamos, Samantha R.
Before you were here, mi amor / by Samantha R. Vamos ; illustrated by Santiago Cohen.
p. cm.
Summary: Family members lovingly prepare for arrival of a new baby.
Spanish words are woven throughout the text.
ISBN 978-0-670-06301-7 (hardcover)
[1. Babies—Fiction. 2. Family life—Fiction. 3. Spanish language—Vocabulary.] I. Cohen, Santiago, ill. II. Title.
PZ7.V2565Be 2009
[E]-dc22
2008021548

Manufactured in China   Set in Tonic

For Jackson, Michael, Travis, and Olivia with love.
With gratitude and love to my mom, who has encouraged me in
every endeavor and especially with respect to my writing.   —S.R.V.

A Ethel, mi amor, gracias por hacerme padre. —S.C.

Before you were here, you lived
in *mi barriguita*, sleeping, eating,
and growing for nine months.

Before you were here, I drank *mucha leche*, and ate *arroz y frijoles* with fish or chicken and *fruta* like papaya, mango, and bananas so you would be healthy and strong.

Before you were here, *tu papi* carved a *mecedora* from the wood of an old walnut tree so you and I could rock and cuddle together.

On warm summer evenings, we swung on the
back porch swing, sharing a bowl of *cerezas*
and writing a list of baby names.

Before you were here, *tu hermano* often asked,
"When will the *bebé* be here?" and "When will
the *bebé* be old enough to play *beísbol* with me?"

Tu hermana drew pictures of *nuestra familia* to show you who everyone is.

Before you were here, *tu abuelo* planted a little *árbol* outside *nuestra casa* to grow along with you.

Your *abuela* painted *un cocodrilo, dos elefantes, tres tigres, cuatro jirafas,* and *cinco monos* on your bedroom wall so you could imagine playing in a tropical jungle.

Before you were here, I danced with you
to the rhythms and *música de salsa.*

Tu tío cooked *arroz con leche* for me to eat so you would have "a sweet and gentle nature."

Before you were here, I felt your tiny *pies* flutter and kick as you moved around inside me.

Tu abuelo felt you kick and said, "*Mi nieto* will play *fútbol.*"

Tu abuela felt you kick and said, "*Mi nieta* will dance flamenco."

Before you were here, *tu hermana*
placed her face against *mi barriguita*
and whispered, *"¡Hola, bebé!"*

Tu papi recited *poesía cantada* while strumming *su guitarra*. "Just in case the *bebé* is listening," he said, with a twinkle in his eyes.

Before you were here, *tu tía* made a *móvil* to hang above your crib. *Triángulos verdes y azules, estrellas moradas y amarillas, lunas naranjas y negras,* and *círculos rojos y blancos* dangled for you to watch.

Tu tío built a small wooden step stool so you could reach the sink to brush your *dientes* and wash your *manos y cara.*

Before you were here, *Papi* and I heard your *corazón* beating at the doctor's office. We made a tape recording and the whole *familia* came to listen. Your heartbeat was *rápido* and strong, and everyone laughed when *nuestro perrito* barked at its sound.

Before you were here, *tu hermana y hermano* filled your bedroom bookcase with some of their favorite *libros*. *Tu papi* hung a shelf for your toys and stuffed animals.

Tu tío brought the bassinet down from the attic, and *tu tía* placed a *conejito* with *dos orejas* and *ojos rosados* inside for you to hug.

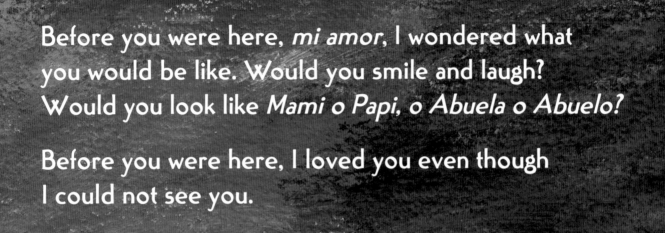

Before you were here, *mi amor*, I wondered what you would be like. Would you smile and laugh? Would you look like *Mami o Papi, o Abuela o Abuelo?*

Before you were here, I loved you even though I could not see you.

And then you were born.

And our waiting was over.

And now we know how wonderful you are.

GLOSSARY

abuela	grandmother	cereza	cherry
abuelo	grandfather	cinco	five
amarillo/amarilla	yellow	círculo	circle
amor	love	cocodrilo	crocodile
árbol	tree	conejito	bunny
arroz	rice	corazón	heart
arroz con leche	rice with milk	cuatro	four
	(rice pudding)	dientes	teeth
azul	blue	dos	two
barriguita	tummy	elefante	elephant
bebé	baby	estrella	star
beísbol	baseball	familia	family
blanco/blanca	white	frijoles	beans
cara	face	fruta	fruit
casa	house	fútbol	soccer
		guitarra	guitar
		hermana	sister
		hermano	brother
		hola	hello
		jirafa	giraffe
		leche	milk

ojos   eyes
orejas   ears
papi   daddy, dad

libro   book
luna   moon
mami   mommy, mom
manos   hands
mecedora   rocking chair
mi   my
mono   monkey
morado/morada   purple
móvil   mobile
mucha   a lot of, much
música de salsa   salsa music
naranja   orange
negro/negra   black
nieta   granddaughter
nieto   grandson
nuestra/nuestro   our
o   or

perrito   puppy
pies   feet
poesía cantada   sung poetry
rápido   fast, quick
rojo/roja   red
rosado/rosada   pink
su   his, her, their
tía   aunt
tigre   tiger
tío   uncle
tres   three
triángulo   triangle
tu   your
un/uno   one
verde   green
y   and